LEGO® CITY

3,2,1 LIFTOFF!

By Sonia Sander
Illustrated by The Artifact Group

SCHOLASTIC INC.

NEW YORK   TORONTO   LONDON   AUCKLAND

SYDNEY   MEXICO CITY   NEW DELHI   HONG KONG

ISBN 978-0-545-33167-8

LEGO, the LEGO logo, the Brick and Knob configurations and the Minifigure are trademark of the LEGO Group. ©2011 The LEGO Group. Produced by Scholastic Inc. under license from the LEGO Group

Designed by Angela Jun

Printed in the U.S.A.
First printing, August 2011

18 17

15/0

40

Before the shuttle can blast off, it has to be looked over.

Vroom!
A big crawler gives the shuttle
a ride.

At the launch pad, the shuttle is loaded up.
It is ready for its special space mission.

The crew gets dressed for take off. Hurry up!

The crew is on their way.
It is time for them to board.

Ten! Nine! Eight! Seven! Six! The countdown clock is ticking. It is almost time to blast off.

Five! Four! Three! Two! One!
Kaboom!
The shuttle lifts off.

Roar!
The shuttle flies up, up, and away.
It races toward outer space.

The shuttle can now fly by itself.
Boom! Boom!
The two boosters fall off.

Splash!
The boosters land in the water.

Crews come and scoop them up.
The boosters can be used again.

Deep in space, nothing holds the crew down.
They float, flip, and fly inside the shuttle.

There is work to be done, too.
The crew helps a satellite fly in
space.

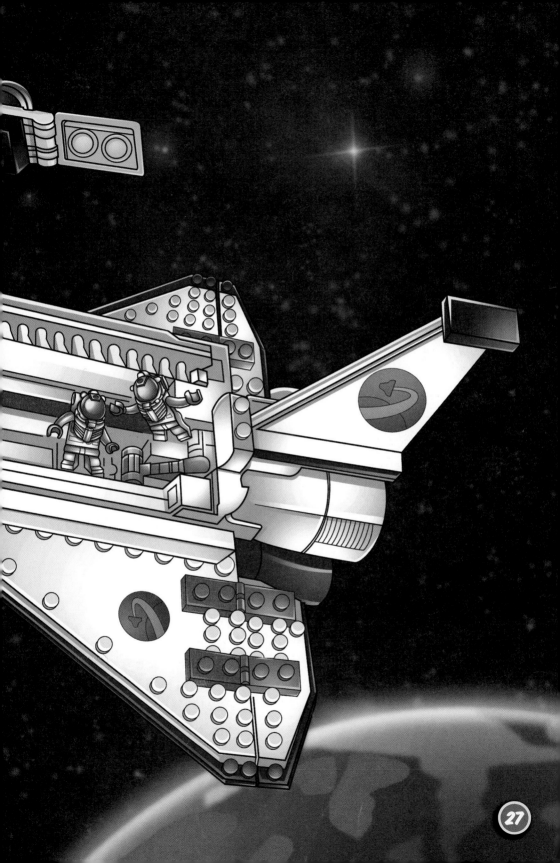

Look! There is the space station.
The shuttle flies toward it.
It very slowly docks to the station.
Click!

There is still a lot to do before the trip back home.
For now, it is time to get some *Zzzzzzz!*

BUILD YOUR LEGO® LIBRARY!

■SCHOLASTIC

www.scholastic.com
www.LEGO.com

LEGOCTY32